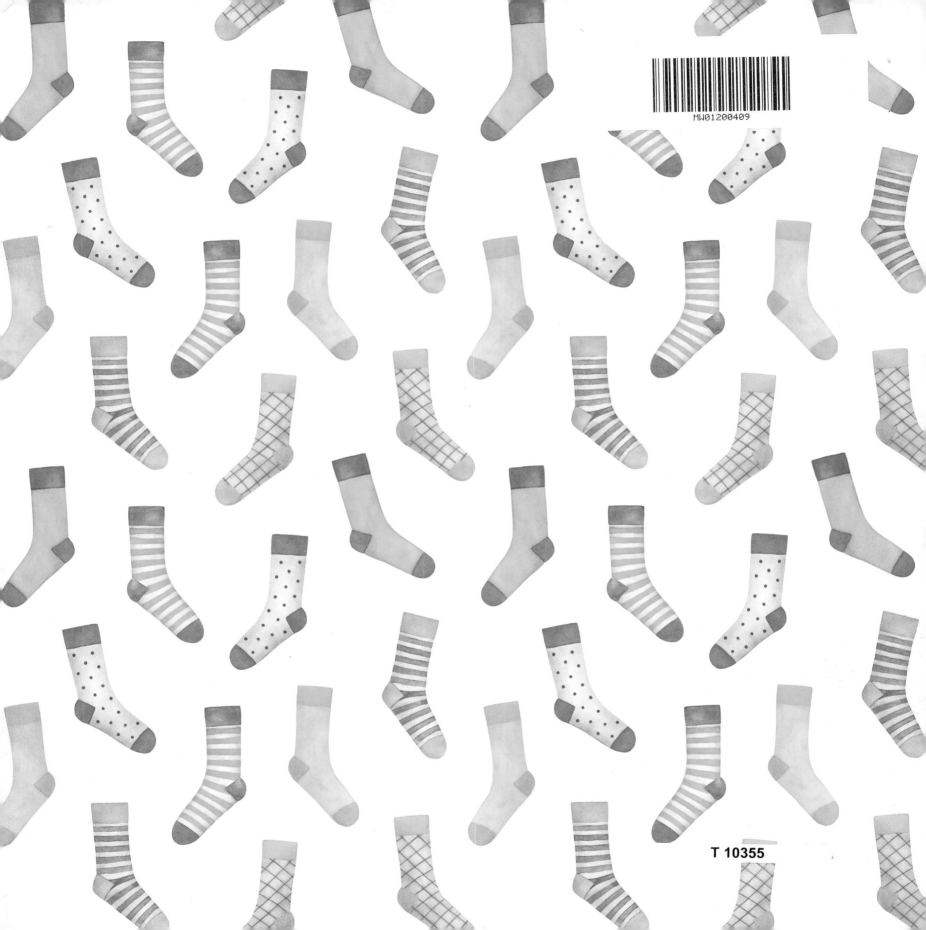

MW01200409

T 10355

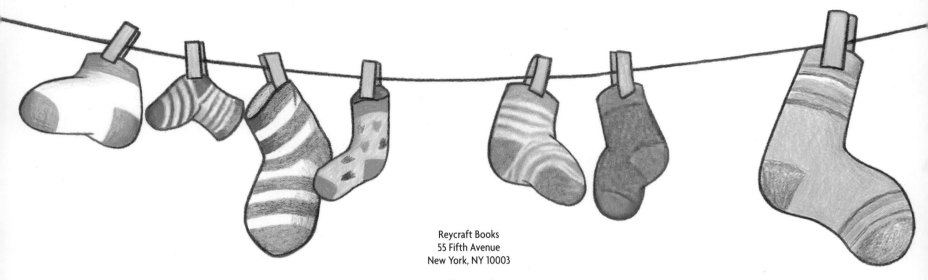

Reycraft Books
55 Fifth Avenue
New York, NY 10003

Reycraftbooks.com

Reycraft Books is a trade imprint and trademark of Newmark Learning, LLC.

This edition is published by arrangement with China Children's Press & Publication Group, China.
© China Children's Press & Publication Group

All rights reserved. No portion of this book may be reproduced, stored in a retrieval
system, or transmitted in any form or by any means, electronic, mechanical, photocopying,
recording, or otherwise, without written permission from the publisher. For information regarding
permission, please contact info@reycraftbooks.com.

Educators and Librarians: Our books may be purchased in bulk for promotional,
educational, or business use. Please contact sales@reycraftbooks.com.

This is a work of fiction. Names, characters, places, dialogue, and incidents described either are
the product of the author's imagination or are used fictitiously. Any resemblance to actual
persons, living or dead, is entirely coincidental.

Sale of this book without a front cover or jacket may be unauthorized. If this book is
coverless, it may have been reported to the publisher as "unsold or destroyed" and
may have deprived the author and publisher of payment.

Library of Congress Cataloging-in-Publication Data is available.

ISBN: 978-1-4788-6805-7

Printed in Guangzhou, China
4401/0919/CA21901483

10 9 8 7 6 5 4 3 2 1

First Edition Hardcover published by Reycraft Books 2019

Reycraft Books and Newmark Learning, LLC, support diversity and
the First Amendment, and celebrate the right to read.

Little Koko Bear
and His Socks

by Qiusheng Zhang · illustrated by Kaiyun Xu

Little Koko Bear loved socks.

Striped socks, polka-dot socks, socks
with hearts—Koko Bear loved them all.

"Socks! Socks! Socks!" sang Koko Bear.

"Socks are what I like to wear.

Red socks, blue socks, I don't care."

"Do you like my brand-new pair?"

Little Koko Bear spent all his time thinking about socks, looking at socks, and trying on socks.

He was so busy with his socks that he didn't have any time left to make friends.

But there was ONE thing Koko Bear didn't like about his socks.

He didn't like washing them.

So, after he wore a pair of socks, little Koko Bear would toss them under his bed.

After a while, there was a big pile of dirty, stinky socks under his bed.

Then one morning, Koko
Bear woke up to find that
he didn't have a single
clean pair of socks to wear.

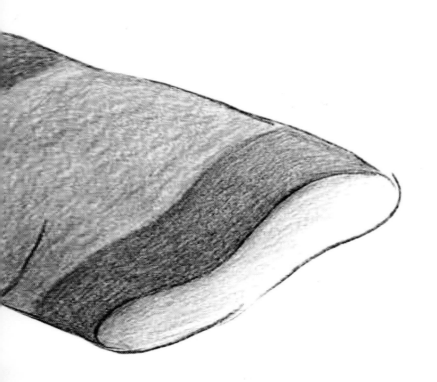
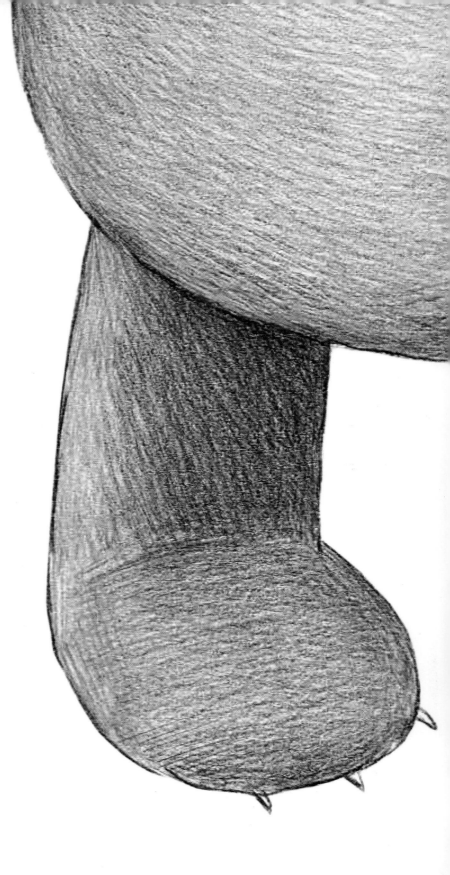

There was no getting around it.

His socks had to be washed.

Little Koko Bear put all his socks in a basket and carried them down to the river.

Dirty socks, dirty socks, everywhere. Not a single sock to wear.

When he was done washing them, Koko Bear hung up his socks to dry. All that work had made him very tired. He lay down under a tree and fell fast asleep.

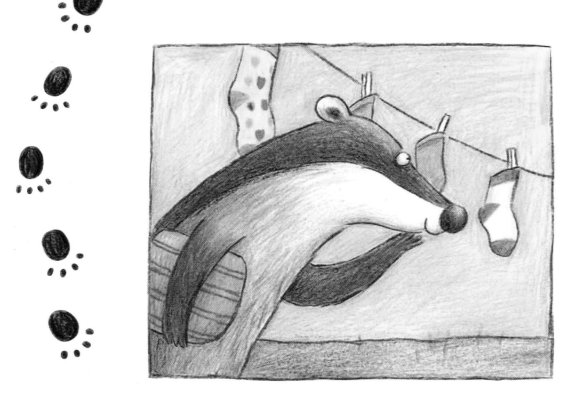

While Koko Bear slept, a friendly badger passed by.

"Look!" she said to herself. "This little bear is selling socks. I don't want to wake him up, but I do need socks. I will take some and pay with the cookies I baked this morning."

So the badger took a few pairs of socks and left behind her delicious cookies.

Koko Bear slept on. A while later,
a cheerful chimpanzee wandered by.

"Oh, look at that!" said the chimpanzee.
"This little bear is selling socks.
I don't want to wake him, but I do
need socks. I'll take some and leave
my fresh apples."

So the chimp took a pair of socks and left
his crisp, juicy apples for Koko Bear.

Little Koko Bear snoozed on. Soon an artist passed by.

"How beautiful!" the artist said. "These socks are like works of art! I don't want to wake him, but I do need socks. I'll take some and paint his picture as payment."

So the artist painted a picture of little Koko Bear and left it next to the cookies and the apples. Then he went away, taking two pairs of socks with him.

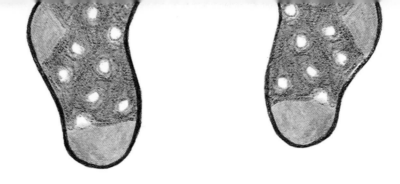

Soon, all the animals in the forest heard that a sleeping bear was selling cheerful, colorful socks. Everyone rushed to get a pair or two.

They all left behind something special for Koko Bear.

Later that afternoon, Koko Bear woke up.
He opened his eyes. He looked up and down.
He looked all around.

Where were his socks?

Only two pairs of socks were left
on the line.

Where were his polka-dot socks?

Where were his heart socks?

Little Koko Bear wanted to cry.

But then he noticed all the
wonderful gifts.

Koko Bear packed the two pairs of socks in his basket along with all the gifts and headed back home.

Now that Koko Bear had only two pairs of socks, he had to wash them at the river almost every day. But he didn't mind. He no longer hated washing socks. Instead, he enjoyed being at the river and talking to the animals he met. He made many new friends.

Little Koko Bear invited his new friends to come over.

He was proud of his house now that there weren't any smelly socks under his bed.

Happy, happy Koko Bear!
Now he has
clean socks to wear.
He's got tasty snacks to share.
And plenty of
good friends who care.

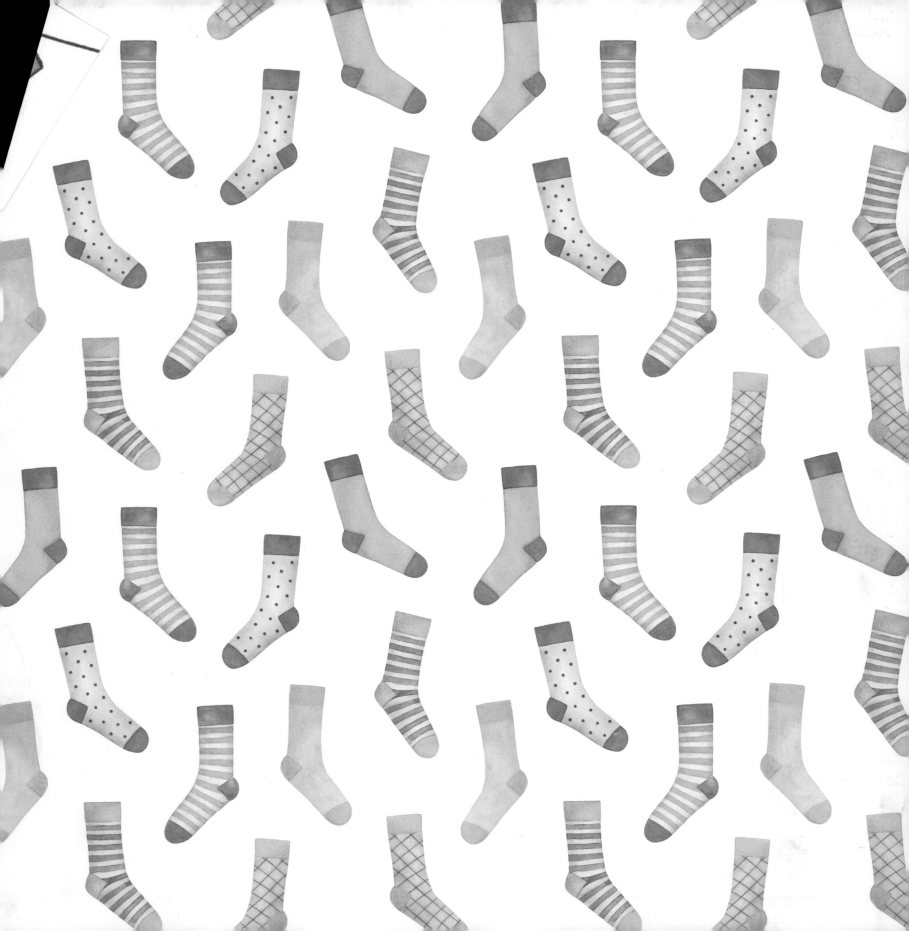